INSIDE MLS

SAN JOSE
EARTHQUAKES

BY SAM MOUSSAVI

SportsZone
An Imprint of Abdo Publishing
abdobooks.com

abdobooks.com

Published by Abdo Publishing, a division of ABDO, PO Box 398166, Minneapolis, Minnesota 55439. Copyright © 2022 by Abdo Consulting Group, Inc. International copyrights reserved in all countries. No part of this book may be reproduced in any form without written permission from the publisher. SportsZone™ is a trademark and logo of Abdo Publishing.

Printed in the United States of America, North Mankato, Minnesota
052021
092021

Cover Photo: Chris Brown/Cal Sport Media/Zuma Wire/AP Images
Interior Photos: Matthew Cavanaugh/AP Images, 5; Larry W. Smith/AP Images, 7; Brian Bahr/Allsport/Getty Images Sport/Getty Images, 9, 10, 13; AP Images, 14–15; Todd Warshaw/Getty Images Sport/Getty Images, 17; John Todd/AP Images, 18, 27, 35; Doug Benc/Getty Images Sport/Getty Images, 21; Damon Tarver/Cal Sport Media/AP Images, 23; Michael Caulfield/AP Images, 25; Dino Vournas/AP Images, 28; Jeff Chiu/AP Images, 31; George Holland/Cal Sport Media/AP Images, 32; Stephen Dunn/Getty Images Sport/Getty Images, 37; Mark J. Terrill/AP Images, 38; Graham Hughes/The Canadian Press/AP Images, 41; Chris Brown/Cal Sport Media/AP Images, 42–43

Editor: Patrick Donnelly
Series Designer: Dan Peluso

Library of Congress Control Number: 2020948269

Publisher's Cataloging-in-Publication Data

Names: Moussavi, Sam, author.
Title: San Jose Earthquakes / by Sam Moussavi
Description: Minneapolis, Minnesota : Abdo Publishing, 2022 | Series: Inside MLS | Includes online resources and index.
Identifiers: ISBN 9781532194825 (lib. bdg.) | ISBN 9781098214487 (ebook)
Subjects: LCSH: San Jose Earthquakes (Soccer team)--Juvenile literature. | Soccer teams--Juvenile literature. | Professional sports franchises--Juvenile literature. | Sports Teams--Juvenile literature.
Classification: DDC 796.334--dc23

TABLE OF CONTENTS

CHAPTER 1
A QUAKES FIRST.................... **4**

CHAPTER 2
DATES TO REMEMBER............ **14**

CHAPTER 3
KEY QUAKES....................... **24**

CHAPTER 4
CLUTCH MOMENTS................ **34**

TIMELINE	44
TEAM FACTS	45
GLOSSARY	46
MORE INFORMATION	47
ONLINE RESOURCES	47
INDEX	48
ABOUT THE AUTHOR	48

CHAPTER 1

A QUAKES
FIRST

Changes were in store for the San Jose Earthquakes in 2001. A new ownership group entered the picture just three months before the start of the Major League Soccer (MLS) season. They were determined to turn around a club that hadn't made the playoffs since the league's first season in 1996.

The first change came on the sidelines. San Jose named Frank Yallop head coach just two days before the league's draft. Yallop would be San Jose's fourth coach in five seasons. He was an experienced and savvy leader during his long playing career. The Earthquakes would lean on Yallop's experience to help unite the new players on the roster.

Defender Jeff Agoos, bottom, was one of San Jose's key acquisitions in 2001.

Yallop wasted little time building a strong team in San Jose. The Quakes first focused on strengthening their defense. The team traded with DC United for All-Star defender Jeff Agoos. Then San Jose acquired defender Zak Ibsen from the LA Galaxy. Agoos, a defensive force, had already won two MLS Cups with DC. Ibsen also had championship experience, having won an MLS Cup with Chicago in 1998.

Next Yallop turned his focus to improving the offensive side of his squad. The team signed talented young forward Dwayne De Rosario. He had been scoring in bunches at the level below MLS. San Jose then traded with Tampa Bay for midfielder Manny Lagos.

However, the most important preseason move happened just a few days before the start of the season. It might have been the most important event in team history. On March 29, the Earthquakes finalized a deal to bring in Landon Donovan on a loan. The 19-year-old was one of the most promising young players in the country. He was already a fixture on the US national team. However, after starting his professional career in Germany, he was struggling to find playing time with his club there. Donovan hoped a move home to California could help kickstart his career.

High-scoring forward Dwayne De Rosario, *front*, began his long MLS career with the Earthquakes in 2001.

TURNING IT AROUND

The 2001 season was San Jose's sixth in MLS. Up to that point, the Quakes had never been past the first round of MLS playoffs. The 2000 season was San Jose's worst ever. But the recent moves brought a new feeling of optimism to soccer fans in Northern California.

After losing two of their first three games of the season, the Earthquakes went on a tear. They didn't lose another match for almost two months. The unbeaten streak from mid-April to early July helped them climb in the standings. But another event that summer put the entire league on notice. MLS got a good look at San Jose's skill level during the 2001 All-Star Game in mid-July. Six Quakes were named to the team. That was a record at the time. And the game would be played in San Jose.

San Jose's All-Stars did not disappoint. The fans who packed the stands at Spartan Stadium roared as Donovan scored four goals. Donovan's offensive genius helped him win the game's Most Valuable Player (MVP) award. San Jose's unbeaten stretch and All-Star brilliance established the Earthquakes as one of the top teams in MLS.

San Jose closed out the season going .500 over its final 12 games. Big wins over DC United and the Kansas City Wizards propelled the Quakes to one of the best seasons in team history. Thanks to Agoos and goalkeeper Joe Cannon, San Jose gave up the fewest goals in the league. The team could score, too. Forward Ronald Cerritos led the Quakes with 11 goals, while Lagos came in second with 8.

Landon Donovan raises the MVP trophy he won in front of his hometown fans at the 2001 MLS All-Star Game.

Richard Mulrooney blasts a free kick during the 2001 MLS Cup.

PLAYOFF PUSH

After posting the league's worst record in 2000, San Jose entered 2001 playoffs with the fifth-best record in the league. The fourth-seeded Columbus Crew were no match for the Quakes in the quarterfinals. Donovan scored three times as they swept the series in two games. That set up a best-of-three series with the Miami Fusion in the semifinals.

Miami had finished with the league's best regular-season record. And the Fusion showed their defense was solid in a 1–0 victory to open the series. San Jose had its chances but missed on several late crossing attempts. But the Earthquakes' defense had also played well. That trend carried over to the rematch in San Jose. The Quakes jumped out on Miami in the 16th minute with a goal from Donovan. San Jose's offense sealed the game in the second half with three more goals. The 4–0 victory sent the Quakes back to Miami for the final game of the series. The winner would advance to the MLS Cup.

The final game was tight and pressure-packed. Neither team scored during regulation. That meant extra time would decide the winner. According to the rules of the time, the first goal would end the game. And four minutes into extra time, three San Jose defenders teamed up to provide one of the most memorable moments in team history.

Richard Mulrooney sent in a corner kick from the right. Jimmy Conrad kicked the ball toward the goal. Then Troy Dayak knocked it past Miami goalkeeper Nick Rimando. The play exemplified San Jose's balance in 2001. The golden goal gave

YALLOP HONORED

As San Jose got ready for the 2001 MLS Cup, first-year coach Frank Yallop was named MLS Coach of the Year. He helped San Jose turn its fortunes around after the team posted the league's worst record in 2000.

the Earthquakes the 1–0 win and their first trip to the MLS Cup.

TROPHY TIME

San Jose faced the LA Galaxy in the final game of 2001. The teams knew each other well. Their rivalry was known as the California *Clasico*. The name was a play on the famed competition between Spanish giants Real Madrid and FC Barcelona. The MLS Cup was played at a neutral field in Columbus, Ohio. The Quakes fell behind early, but Donovan tied it just before halftime with a deft one-touch goal off a cross. The right-footed strike was Donovan's fifth of the playoffs. It capped a phenomenal first season in MLS.

After a scoreless second half, a sudden-death extra time period began. Six minutes later, De Rosario handled a long pass, dribbled a bit, and unleashed a right-footed shot. The ball bent just past the outstretched hands of the Galaxy keeper and found the net. De Rosario's golden goal had given San Jose its first MLS Cup. After five seasons of struggles, the Earthquakes were able to call themselves champions.

The Earthquakes celebrate their first MLS Cup victory.

CHAPTER 2

DATES TO REMEMBER

The Earthquakes were charter members of MLS. But their roots trace back to a different pro league two decades earlier. In 1974 San Jose was awarded a franchise in the North American Soccer League (NASL). The *San Jose Mercury News* held a contest for fans to name the team. Many entries were considered. "Earthquakes" was a fitting nickname due to San Jose's location near the famous San Andreas Fault.

The Earthquakes got off to a decent start. They made the playoffs in three of their first four seasons. They even won the Southern Division and reached the conference finals in 1976. But the Quakes were mostly stuck in last place over their final eight seasons, making just one playoff appearance.

Earthquakes goalkeeper Mike Hewitt leaps to make a save against the Minnesota Kicks during a 1976 NASL playoff game.

The NASL folded after the 1984 season, but that was not the end of pro soccer in the South Bay. The Earthquakes bounced around in a couple of minor leagues for the next few years. The popularity of soccer and strong fan support were clear in San Jose. The Quakes just needed a stronger league to play in. Finally, in the early 1990s, plans were being set to create MLS. The league would begin play in 1996. Two years prior, MLS announced San Jose would be among the 10 teams. However, the league and its sponsors wanted a fresh start. So San Jose's team was named the Clash, rather than the Earthquakes, at the start of its MLS rebirth.

HERE COME THE CLASH

The San Jose Clash hosted the first-ever MLS game on April 6, 1996. The Clash's Eric Wynalda, a star on the US national team, scored the first goal in MLS history. San Jose held on to defeat DC United 1–0. Later that season, the team made history again. A match against the LA Galaxy—their California *Clasico* rival—drew 31,728 people to Spartan Stadium in San Jose. That set the record for attendance at a sporting event in the city of San Jose.

Though the Clash made the playoffs in 1996, the team failed to qualify for the postseason the next four seasons. Those early

A packed house at Spartan Stadium witnessed the first game in MLS history on April 6, 1996.

seasons were not a waste, however. Soccer historians look to the 1999 season as a major building block for the 2001 MLS title run. San Jose made several key additions to its roster that year. Defender Richard Mulrooney and goalkeeper Joe Cannon were among those who made their debuts in 1999. They and a handful of other players would form the core of the first generation of San Jose stars.

Joe Cannon became a steady presence in the net for the Quakes.

The 2000 season saw the return of the Earthquakes nickname. The popular switch was a nod to the team's NASL roots. But the name change meant little in the standings, as San Jose missed the playoffs again. The team did continue its development for the future, however. Cannon emerged as a force, serving as a bright spot during an otherwise tough season. He was in net for seven of the Earthquakes' nine shutouts during that year.

All the pieces fell into place in 2001 when San Jose won the MLS Cup. That meant they began the next season in an unfamiliar position as league favorites. Most of the championship core returned for 2002, as did coach Frank Yallop. Fans expected the Quakes to play well, and they did not disappoint. They improved their win total from 13 to 14 and had the second-most points in the league. But the playoffs were not as kind to the Quakes. The Columbus Crew pulled out a pair of 2–1 victories to defeat San Jose in the first round.

ANOTHER TROPHY

Even with a mostly new roster and handful of key preseason injuries, the Quakes started the 2003 season strong. Top players such as Mulrooney and Landon Donovan missed time with injuries and national team commitments. Overall San Jose's players combined to miss more than 100 games that year.

But the team did not miss a beat. Contributions came from every player on the roster as the team set a new club record for points in a season. The Quakes held onto first place in the Western Conference for all but one week of the regular season.

However, San Jose needed a miracle to escape the first round of the playoffs. Down 4–0 in aggregate against the Galaxy, the Earthquakes battled back to force extra time with a goal in the final minute. Then Donovan set up Rodrigo Faria to score the golden goal six minutes into extra time, allowing the Earthquakes to advance.

MORE MAGIC

Just six days later San Jose began the Western Conference finals against the Kansas City Wizards. A spot in the MLS Cup was on the line. After a scoreless first half, the teams traded goals twice, with the Wizards taking two leads and the Earthquakes quickly tying the score. The match remained level at 2–2 deep into extra time. But just when it appeared a shootout would be necessary, Donovan scored the golden goal and San Jose soared to its second MLS Cup in three seasons.

The 2003 MLS Cup was played in Carson, California, home of the Galaxy. Winning a trophy on their archrivals' field would make it that much sweeter. And it was, as Donovan scored twice to lift San Jose past the Chicago Fire 4–2. The win capped

Rodrigo Faria (22) fights off the Galaxy's Danny Califf during the teams' epic 2003 playoff matchup.

a three-season run in which the Quakes held the league's best win-loss record.

San Jose stumbled to a seventh-place finish the next year. But the 2005 team roared back to earn the Supporters' Shield, given to the team with the best regular season record. All that success was not enough to guarantee pro soccer's place in the South Bay, however. After the 2005 season, the Earthquakes' owner moved the team to Houston. With many of the same players who thrived in San Jose, Houston won the MLS Cup in 2006 and 2007. However, MLS would soon return to the Bay Area.

BACK IN MLS

Early on, most MLS teams played in big football stadiums. As the league grew, it sought more soccer-specific stadiums that were better suited to MLS crowds. And if a new owner emerged with a plan for a stadium in San Jose, the league was eager to come back. That happened in 2007, and the reborn Earthquakes resumed play in 2008. The new

NEW STADIUM

From plans to play it took nearly six years for the Quakes to have their own place to call home. Plans and blueprints for a new soccer-specific stadium near the San Jose airport were unveiled in 2009. Construction began in 2013, and Avaya Stadium opened on March 22, 2015. San Jose defeated Chicago 2–1 in front of a capacity crowd of 18,000 in the first match at the new venue.

The Earthquakes opened Avaya Stadium, now known as Earthquakes Stadium, in 2015.

team took on the history of the old Earthquakes, while the Dynamo were considered a brand-new franchise in Houston.

The Quakes returned to the playoffs in 2010. The 2012 season marked a true renaissance for the team. That squad, known lovingly in San Jose as "The Goonies," set the team record for most wins and points in a season. The Quakes also earned the Supporters' Shield for the second time in team history.

San Jose barely missed the playoffs in 2013. That was the start of a long downturn in the team's fortunes, as the Quakes would play just one playoff game over the next seven seasons. The MLS Cup days were a distant memory as the Earthquakes looked to build another championship contender.

CHAPTER 3

KEY QUAKES

Eric Wynalda was playing in Germany when he got the call. MLS was preparing to restart first-division soccer in the United States, and the league wanted the US national team star to come home.

"The move to Major League Soccer was so important to so many people," Wynalda said. "It would have been wrong if I didn't come home."

Wynalda ended up joining the Clash. The move proved to be an important one, both for the league and the team. Wynalda had already played in two World Cups. Fans knew him as a player willing to speak his mind—and able to score lots of goals. His arrival instantly brought star power to San Jose.

Eric Wynalda (11) played a huge role for the Clash in the league's early days.

That showed right away in the first MLS game. Organizers were nervous that fans might be slow to embrace the new league. And when the first game in league history remained scoreless as the end of regulation approached, that anxiety grew. Then, in the 88th minute, Wynalda beat a defender and ripped a right-footed shot between two others for a goal. The Clash's biggest star had come through when the team—and the league—needed it. Wynalda ended up playing three seasons in the South Bay and scored 21 goals during that time.

A TRUE LEGEND

Coach Frank Yallop and general manager Tom Neale showed an eye for talent in putting together the Quakes' 2001 team. And when presented with a player who would go on to define the league, they jumped at the chance to sign him.

Landon Donovan arrived in MLS looking to jumpstart his young career. He did that, and then some, in San Jose. As a player, Donovan was known for his versatility and stamina. He always seemed to be around the net, either scoring goals or setting up teammates.

The young star came through in big moments, too. Donovan won the 2003 MLS Cup MVP Award after his two goals

Landon Donovan became a star in San Jose.

helped the Quakes beat Chicago. He also earned a spot on the MLS Best XI squad for the first time that year.

Many US soccer fans were eager for Donovan to leave MLS and try to prove himself back in Europe. Instead Donovan

Troy Dayak scored some huge goals for San Jose over the years.

played most of his career in MLS. In doing so, he is often credited with helping the league grow and establish itself. Donovan left San Jose after the 2004 season and went on to become one of the league's iconic players with the Galaxy. In total he won six MLS Cups across 15 seasons, a league record.

The league even named its MVP award after him. Donovan also holds the MLS career assists record with 136.

HOMETOWN HERO

Troy Dayak was a staple in the Bay Area soccer world even before MLS existed. Dayak grew up in nearby Walnut Creek, and he played for minor league teams based in San Francisco and San Jose from 1989 to 1995. When MLS began in 1996, the teams held a draft to assemble their rosters. Dayak was chosen by the New York/New Jersey MetroStars in the first round. However, he refused to join the MetroStars and was traded to the Clash before the season.

As a defender, Dayak was known for always being around the ball. But his physical play led to problems, too. After he suffered a serious neck injury in 1998, doctors told Dayak he might never play again. But Dayak did not give up. He went through a grueling cycle of surgeries, rehab, and minor league action without any guarantee of a spot on an MLS roster. That all changed in 2001 when Yallop chose Dayak for a spot on the Quakes.

After scoring the golden goal against Miami in 2001 playoffs, Dayak took home the MLS Comeback Player of the Year Award. He was a key figure on both of San Jose's championship teams and played a total of eight seasons for his hometown club.

THE GOAL-SCORING GOAT

Earthquakes midfielder Shea Salinas dribbled the ball inside the corner of the penalty area. Chris Wondolowski knew just what to do. The veteran striker waited near the far post. And when Salinas send a hard pass his way, "Wondo" slid just enough to knock the ball into the net. It was his 145th career goal, tying the MLS record set by Donovan. And much to the Chicago Fire's dismay on May 18, 2019, he was just getting started.

In the 48th minute, Chicago's goalkeeper misplayed an easy save. Wondolowski was right there to knock in the rebound and take record for himself. He beat the keeper again with a well-placed shot for the hat trick 26 minutes later. And then two minutes after that, he tapped in his fourth goal from a wide-open position on the back post.

The Earthquakes had selected Wondolowski in the 2005 MLS Supplemental Draft. But the Danville, California, native made only two appearances for San Jose before the team moved to Houston. Wondolowski returned to the South Bay in 2009 in a trade after winning two MLS Cups as a role player

Chris Wondolowski is mobbed by his teammates after setting the record for most career MLS goals.

Wondolowski carried the Earthquakes to the top of the league during his MVP season of 2012.

with Houston. Once he returned home and started getting regular playing time, Wondolowski became the greatest scorer in MLS history.

His breakout campaign came in 2010, when he scored 18 goals for San Jose and was a finalist for the league MVP award. It was the first of 10 straight seasons with double-digit goals for Wondolowski. He won the MVP award in 2012 after scoring 27 goals. His efforts that season helped the Quakes earn the MLS Supporters' Shield.

Wondolowski planned to retire following the 2020 season. However, after that season was disrupted and played mostly without fans in attendance due to the COVID-19 pandemic, he signed another one-year contract.

"The fans have consistently supported me through the ups and downs," he said, "and I'd always regret not properly saying goodbye."

FRANK YALLOP

Frank Yallop had developed an eye for talent during a long playing career in England and MLS. That showed during his two runs as coach in San Jose. Yallop led the Quakes to MLS Cup wins in 2001 and 2003. After stints coaching the Canadian national team and the rival Galaxy, he came back to San Jose in 2008 to lead the reborn Quakes. In nine seasons, he led San Jose to two MLS Cups, the 2012 Supporters' Shield, and five postseason berths. He was named MLS Coach of the Year twice before leaving San Jose midway through 2013.

CHAPTER 4

CLUTCH MOMENTS

After the 2002 Earthquakes failed to defend their MLS title, the team experienced a massive roster turnover. Shaking things up further, star forward Dwayne De Rosario tore a knee ligament while training. He was expected to miss the entire 2003 season.

But responding to adversity was nothing new to Frank Yallop and his squad. Yallop built the roster with the depth to deal with injuries and the experience to handle increased expectations. And when Landon Donovan also missed time with injuries, teammates were ready to step up.

Of the nine new faces on the team, rookies Todd Dunivant and Jamil Walker impressed the most. Walker scored four

From left, Landon Donovan, Ronnie Ekelund, and Dwayne De Rosario embrace after Donovan scored a goal in 2003.

goals in 19 appearances off the bench, while Dunivant played solid defense and chipped in three assists.

Fellow newcomers Brian Mullan and Brian Ching set personal career highs with six goals apiece. Pat Onstad took over at goalie for Joe Cannon and set several Quakes records in the process. Onstad was named MLS Goalkeeper of Year and joined Donovan on the MLS Best XI team.

All that depth gave De Rosario and Donovan the time necessary to return to complete health. Donovan missed five weeks, while De Rosario didn't make his season debut until August 8. But both forwards notched hat tricks that season—the first two such feats in Quakes history.

COMEBACK CITY

The Quakes made more history in the playoffs with an astonishing comeback. Entering the postseason as the top seed in the Western Conference, San Jose faced the rival LA Galaxy in a two-game series. The Earthquakes dropped the first match on the road 2–0. Then, back in San Jose for the second leg, the Galaxy struck twice in the first 13 minutes.

Facing a 4–0 deficit in aggregate, the Quakes didn't give up. First, Jeff Agoos scored off a free kick. Then Donovan scored

Quakes coach Frank Yallop responds to the fans after the thrilling playoff series against the Galaxy.

Donovan and De Rosario celebrate a goal in the 2003 MLS Cup.

to cut the deficit to two before halftime. In the 50th minute, Walker scored on a header off a free kick by Richard Mulrooney to pull San Jose within a goal. Onstad made a handful of amazing stops to keep the Galaxy off the scoreboard.

Meanwhile, the Earthquakes kept pressing, and their efforts finally paid off in the 90th minute. After a great individual effort to create some space, Mulrooney served up another cross into the box. This time, defender Chris Roner—who had subbed into the match two minutes earlier—leaped high to head it home, tying the aggregate score 4–4.

That set up a sudden-death extra time. The first team to score would advance to the second round. And six minutes in, Donovan feathered a pass ahead to Rodrigo Faria, who beat the weary Galaxy defense and drilled a shot past the LA keeper. One of the greatest comebacks in league history was complete.

San Jose was back at it just six days later at Spartan Stadium against the Kansas City Wizards. Once again, the Quakes fell behind. San Jose fought back from two one-goal deficits in the second half. After Mullan's goal tied the game 2–2 in the 83rd minute, extra time was needed to decide which club would earn a spot in the MLS Cup.

It was Donovan's turn to shine, as he had time and time again. The young American sealed the win with a golden goal with just three minutes to go in extra time.

The MLS Cup brought a showdown against the Chicago Fire. This time, finally, the Quakes started strong. After taking a 2–0 lead on goals from Ronnie Ekelund and Donovan, San Jose won 4–2 to claim its second league title in three seasons.

SHIELD WINNERS

The Quakes earned Supporters' Shields in 2005 and 2012. Each team did so in very different fashions.

In 2005 the Quakes were rebuilding after the loss of several key players from the successful squads of the early 2000s. Head coach Dominic Kinnear's team was dominant nonetheless, posting a plus-22 goal differential. Led by Onstad, San Jose's defense was the stingiest in the league as well.

Though the 2005 team was eliminated in the first round of the playoffs, the Quakes set several team highs. The club records for longest winning streak, longest road winning streak, most road wins, and most shutouts fell in 2005. San Jose also finished the regular season unbeaten at home.

Goalkeeper Jon Busch helped lead the 2012 Quakes to the best record in the league.

On the other hand, the 2012 Supporters' Shield team, led again by Yallop, was known for its tenacity and resiliency. The grittiness of the team was exemplified by its nickname, "the Goonies."

The Goonies was a popular film from the 1980s in which the main characters scream the line, "Goonies never say die!" The same line became the rallying cry for the 2012 Earthquakes. The team, led by league MVP Chris Wondolowski, refused

The sun sets on Stanford Stadium, where more than 50,000 fans watched the Quakes shut out the Galaxy 3–0 on June 29, 2019.

to give up. The Quakes made a habit of coming back late in matches to win or at least draw.

The Goonies rewrote the team record books again in 2012. They broke the records for most wins and points that had been set in 2005. Additionally, Wondolowski tied the MLS record for most goals in a season with 27.

San Jose fell short once again in the 2012 playoffs, however. The team lost a heartbreaker in aggregate to the rival Galaxy. Though Yallop's squad fell short of winning a third MLS Cup, they brought the joy and excitement back to the Bay Area.

Some lean years followed, but a new era began when Matias Almeyda was hired as coach in 2019. His boom-or-bust Quakes returned to the playoffs the next year, bringing hope once again to the South Bay's soccer fans.

RECORD CROWD

Though the Earthquakes hit a dry spell after 2012, their fans did not desert them. On June 29, 2019, the LA Galaxy headed north to resume the California *Clasico* rivalry. This time, however, the Quakes moved the game to Stanford Stadium, a bit northwest of their home but still in the South Bay. A crowd of 50,850 showed up, the largest ever for a California *Clasico* match. The home team responded with a resounding 3–0 victory.

TIMELINE

1994
On June 15, the San Jose Clash are founded as an MLS charter club.

1996
On April 6, Eric Wynalda scores the only goal as the Clash win the first MLS regular-season match 1–0 over DC United.

1999
On October 27, the team changes its nickname to the Earthquakes to honor the team that played in the NASL from 1974 to 1984.

2001
On October 21, the Earthquakes defeat the LA Galaxy 2–1 in Columbus, Ohio, to win their first MLS Cup.

2003
On November 9, San Jose overcomes a 4–0 aggregate deficit against the Galaxy to reach their second MLS Cup.

2003
On November 23, the Earthquakes defeat Chicago 4–2 in Carson, California, to win their second MLS Cup.

2005
The Quakes finish with the league's best record to earn the MLS Supporters' Shield.

2008
The reborn Earthquakes return to MLS play after the original squad had moved to Houston to become the Dynamo two years earlier.

2015
On March 22, the Earthquakes open Avaya Stadium with a 2–1 victory over the Chicago Fire.

2019
On May 18, Chris Wondolowski scores four goals against Chicago to set the MLS career goal-scoring record.

TEAM FACTS

FIRST SEASON
1996

STADIUMS
Spartan Stadium (1996–05)
Buck Shaw Stadium (2008–14)
Earthquakes Stadium (2015–)

MLS CUP TITLES
2001, 2003

SUPPORTERS' SHIELDS
2005, 2012

KEY PLAYERS
Jeff Agoos (2001–04)
Joe Cannon (1999–2002, 2008–10)
Dwayne De Rosario (2001–05)
Landon Donovan (2001–04)
John Doyle (1996–2000)
Richard Mulrooney (1999–2004)
Pat Onstad (2003–05)
Andrew Tarbell (2016–)
Chris Wondolowski (2005, 2009–)
Eric Wynalda (1996–99)

KEY COACHES
Dominic Kinnear (2004–05, 2015–17)
Frank Yallop (2001–03, 2008–13)

MLS MOST VALUABLE PLAYER
Chris Wondolowski (2012)

MLS DEFENDER OF THE YEAR
Jeff Agoos (2001)
John Doyle (1996)

MLS NEWCOMER OF THE YEAR
Darren Huckerby (2008)

MLS GOALKEEPER OF THE YEAR
Joe Cannon (2002)
Pat Onstad (2003, 2005)

MLS HUMANITARIAN OF THE YEAR
Abdul Thompson Conteh (2000)

MLS COMEBACK PLAYER OF THE YEAR
Brian Ching (2004)
Bobby Convey (2010)
Troy Dayak (2001)

MLS COACH OF THE YEAR
Dominic Kinnear (2005)
Frank Yallop (2001, 2012)

GLOSSARY

aggregate
The combined score of both games in a two-game series.

charter
Belonging to a group in its first year of existence.

deft
Quick and skillful.

franchise
A sports organization, including the top-level team and all minor league affiliates.

goal differential
The difference between the number of goals scored and goals allowed.

golden goal
A goal scored in extra time to win a game under a sudden-death format.

hat trick
Three goals by the same player in one game.

postseason
Another word for playoffs; the time after the end of the regular season when teams play to determine a champion.

savvy
Able to make good judgements.

shutout
A game in which one team does not score.

stamina
The ability to sustain prolonged physical or mental effort.

MORE INFORMATION

BOOKS

Hewson, Anthony K. *Houston Dynamo*. Minneapolis, MN: Abdo Publishing, 2022.

Marthaler, Jon. *Ultimate Soccer Road Trip*. Minneapolis, MN: Abdo Publishing, 2019.

Trusdell, Brian. *Soccer Record Breakers*. Minneapolis, MN: Abdo Publishing, 2016.

ONLINE RESOURCES

To learn more about the San Jose Earthquakes, please visit **abdobooklinks.com** or scan this QR code. These links are routinely monitored and updated to provide the most current information available.

INDEX

Agoos, Jeff, 6, 8, 36
Almeyda, Matias, 43
Cannon, Joe, 8, 17, 19, 36
Cerritos, Ronald, 8
Ching, Brian, 36
Conrad, Jimmy, 11
Dayak, Troy, 11, 29–30
De Rosario, Dwayne, 6, 12, 34–36
Donovan, Landon, 6, 8, 10–12, 19–20, 26–29, 30, 34–36, 39–40
Dunivant, Todd, 34–36

Ekelund, Ronnie, 40
Faria, Rodrigo, 20, 39
Ibsen, Zak, 6
Kinnear, Dominic, 40
Lagos, Manny, 6, 8
Mullan, Brian, 36, 39
Mulrooney, Richard, 11, 17, 19, 39
Neale, Tom, 26
Onstad, Pat, 36, 39, 40

Rimando, Nick, 11
Roner, Chris, 39
Salinas, Shea, 30
Walker, Jamil, 34–36, 39
Wondolowski, Chris, 30, 33, 41–42
Wynalda, Eric, 16, 24–26
Yallop, Frank, 4–6, 12, 19, 26, 29, 33, 34, 41–42

ABOUT THE AUTHOR

Sam Moussavi is a novelist and freelance writer based in the San Francisco Bay area.